THE AMAZING LIFE OF
MARY, QUEEN OF SCOTS

To George Harris, with thanks, and in memory of
Jean Plaidy and Dorothy Dunnett, who helped me
understand that history is about people – G.A.

For Ben, Hannah and Olivia – M.P.

Kelpies is an imprint of Floris Books
First published in 2021 by Floris Books

Text © 2021 Gill Arbuthnott
Series concept and illustrations © 2021 Floris Books
Gill Arbuthnott and Mike Phillips have asserted their rights
under the Copyright, Designs and Patent Act 1988
to be identified as the Author and Illustrator of this Work

 Also available as an eBook

British Library CIP data available
ISBN 978-178250-668-3
Printed & bound by MBM Print SCS Ltd, Glasgow

MIX
Paper from
responsible sources
FSC® C117931
www.fsc.org

Floris Books supports sustainable forest management
by printing this book on materials made from wood that
comes from responsible sources and reclaimed material

FACT-TASTIC STORIES FROM SCOTLAND'S HISTORY

THE AMAZING LIFE OF MARY, QUEEN OF SCOTS

WRITTEN BY GILL ARBUTHNOTT

ILLUSTRATED BY MIKE PHILLIPS

Young Kelpies

MEET THE PEOPLE IN MARY'S STORY

Mary

The Four Marys

David Rizzio

James Stuart

Earl of Bothwell

Francis II

Lord Darnley

Alec, Janet, Walter and Isabelle are characters who could have existed in Mary's story. All the others really did exist.

Alec

Janet

Walter

Isabelle

Mary, Queen of Scots

1542   Mary born; her father dies

1543   Mary crowned Queen of Scotland

1548   Mary smuggled out of Scotland to France

1559   Mary and Francis II become King and Queen of France

1560   Francis dies

1561   Mary returns to Scotland

1565   Mary marries Lord Darnley

1566   Mary gives birth to James

1567   Lord Darnley murdered; Mary marries Earl of Bothwell; Mary imprisoned; James crowned king

1568   Mary escapes, but after Langside defeat she flees to England and is held prisoner there

1586   Mary stands trial for treason

1587   Mary executed

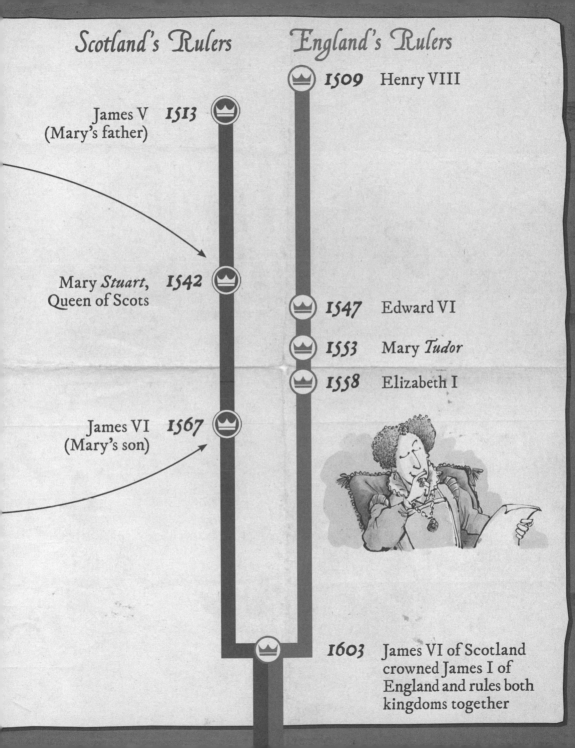

Scotland's Rulers

1513 James V
(Mary's father)

1542 Mary *Stuart,*
Queen of Scots

1567 James VI
(Mary's son)

England's Rulers

1509 Henry VIII

1547 Edward VI

1553 Mary *Tudor*

1558 Elizabeth I

1603 James VI of Scotland
crowned James I of
England and rules both
kingdoms together

1. THE RETURN OF THE QUEEN

Palace of Holyroodhouse, Edinburgh, Scotland
August 1561

"What's she like?"

Everyone in the kitchen wanted to know.

"Beautiful," said the messenger, who had ridden fast from Leith docks. "And tall – right tall for a woman. Red hair – but dark red, not ginger like that wee lad."

Everyone turned and stared at me. I went scarlet and

looked down at the floor, and Janet elbowed me in the ribs.

Usually, no one paid me any attention. A turnspit like me was the lowest of the low. It was my job to keep the big iron spit turning over the fire, so the meat on it cooked properly and didn't burn. At night I slept in a corner of the kitchen, next to the cat. At least it was warm. Much better than the cold streets. And I got plenty of food. Sometimes I could even sneak a taste of grand dishes like roasted pheasant. I once ate some wee gold marzipan flowers. They had fallen and got a bit dirty, so couldn't be used for the banquet.

SWEET TREATS

Sweets were very popular in Mary's time. A favourite was 'marchpane' – what we call marzipan. Some rich people ate so much of it that their teeth rotted and turned black.

I shared my treats with Janet the laundry maid. We were the same age – well, she wasn't sure of her age, but she seemed about ten like me – and we were friends.

The Palace of Holyroodhouse had been in uproar since we heard Queen Mary was on her way home from France. Her husband the French king had died and she was coming home

to Scotland, aged eighteen, to rule her own country.

"And when will she be here?" That was Walter, who was in charge of all the kitchen and serving staff.

"This afternoon."

"Then it's time we all got back to work. Holyroodhouse must be perfect for her."

MARY'S CHILDHOOD

Mary was born in Linlithgow Palace, between Edinburgh and Stirling, in 1542.

JAMES V

Mary's father was King James V of Scotland.

MARY OF GUISE

Mary's mother was a powerful Frenchwoman, Mary of Guise.

Mary's father died when she was just six days old, which meant she became Queen of Scotland when she was only a baby.

The Rough Wooing 1542-1550

As soon as Mary was born, Henry VIII, King of England, wanted her to marry his son, Edward, because that would unite Scotland and England once Edward became king.

EDWARD VI

Henry VIII was a Protestant Christian and he wanted Scotland to become Protestant, like England.

BUT

Mary's French mother was a Catholic Christian. She hoped that Mary would marry a French prince, so Scotland would stay Catholic and have close ties to France.

England declared war on Scotland to force the marriage they wanted. Henry VIII ordered the English troops to:

put all to fire and sword,
burn Edinburgh town,
so razed and defaced when
you have sacked and gotten
what ye can of it, as there
may remain forever a
perpetual memory of
the vengeance of God
lightened upon them!

The war lasted for seven years.

The word 'wooing' means 'courting' or trying to persuade someone to marry you. Wooing traditionally involved giving compliments, sending letters or maybe singing a love song, not fighting. Scottish people called England's war 'the Rough Wooing' because it used fighting to force Mary and the country into accepting Henry VIII's marriage plan.

Moving to France

Young Mary lived in strongholds like Stirling Castle, and she was moved around the country to keep her hidden from the English army. When she was five years old, she was smuggled to France for safety, where she lived with the French royal family. Her mother stayed behind to help govern Scotland while Mary was growing up.

In France, Mary learned many different languages, music, dancing, horse riding, falconry and embroidery.

Mary's First Marriage 1558

FRANCIS II AND MARY

When she was fifteen, Mary married French Prince Francis.

The next year, the French king died, so Francis and Mary became King and Queen of France.

At age sixteen, Mary was Queen of Scotland *and* Queen of France!

Return to Scotland 1561

A year later, Francis died. His younger brother became King of France.

Mary's mother had also died, and eighteen-year-old Mary returned to Scotland to take up her throne.

She arrived in Leith by ship and was met by cheering crowds. The people were delighted to see Mary, and to hear her speak good Scots despite having lived so long in France.

UNWELCOME WELCOME!

Mary was kept awake on her first night in Scotland by not-very-good musicians playing outside the palace!

Palace of Holyroodhouse
3 days later

The feasting and dancing hasn't stopped since Queen Mary arrived. The kitchen has been on the go day and night. Walter came in shouting for more bread and called me over.

"Get some wee bits of roast fowl. The Queen wants some for one of her dogs that's ailing."

I hurried to do as I was told. Walter has been liable to go off like a firework since the Queen's return.

He frowned at me as I stood there holding a bowl of chicken pieces.

"You're an awful sight." He looked round the busy kitchen, which was swarming like a kicked anthill. "But there's no one else can come upstairs. Right. Follow me. Don't speak to anyone. Don't look at anyone. Do as I say and get out of the Queen's chambers as soon as you put that bowl down."

The Queen's chambers. I thought I must have heard him wrong. I hardly ever even got out of the kitchen.

I followed Walter up the stairs, away from the servants' world and into the light and colour of the grand halls.

We came to a lady in a blue dress standing in front of a door. She gave me a look as if I was something nasty she'd found on the sole of her shoe, but she opened the door. I followed Walter into a firelit chamber, bright with candles. There were hangings on the walls, little tables and cushioned chairs. Half a dozen people in fancy clothes sat listening to a dark-haired man playing the lute. I forgot I'd been told not to look at people. I was desperate for a glimpse of the Queen, but none of the ladies had red hair.

"In the corner, over there," said Walter in a low tone, then walked away to set down the tray of wine and glasses he was carrying.

In the corner were two wee white dogs. I went across and put the bowl in front of them. One of them shoved its nose into the dish right away, but the other one just lay there, looking miserable. Walter was still busy, so I stayed where I was and held a bit of chicken out to the sad dog. It got to its feet and took a step towards me, then sank down, whimpering. I stroked its silky head.

"What's the matter, lass? Have you hurt your leg?" I felt along its legs, but there didn't seem to be anything wrong. "Come here. Let me see your paws."

I lifted it onto my knees so I could look at them properly. There was something between the pads of one hind paw that caught the light. I tried to pull it out.

"Ouch!" My finger was bleeding. The poor dog had a splinter of glass stuck in its paw.

"What are you doing?" A woman's voice. I hadn't heard her coming close. Now I was in trouble. I looked up. And up. She was tall, and beautiful, and red haired.

"Y-y-your Majesty," I stammered. "S-s-s-sorry. I meant no harm. There's a bit of glass. In her paw. I-I-I was trying to take it out."

In the next two seconds I imagined myself flung out onto the streets, in jail, executed...

But then Queen Mary was on her knees beside me on the floor.

"Show me," she said, and when I did, she handed me her lace-edged handkerchief. "Here, use this to grip it."

Sure enough, the glass came out easily then. The dog whimpered once, then started to lick the paw.

"Poor Isabelle. She has been so miserable today, but I did not know why." *The Queen was talking to me!* "Thank you. Now she will be better." She waved at Walter to come over. *Oh no...*

"Majesty, my apologies. The lad was told..."

"The lad has been most helpful." She handed Walter the piece of glass. "Throw this in the fire."

He bowed.

"Louis, you have had enough." She pulled the other dog away from the dish and pushed the food closer to Isabelle. "What is your name, lad?"

"Alec Leslie, Your Majesty."

"And Walter is your father?"

"No, Your Majesty. My parents are dead."

"Ah... I see. What age are you?"

"Ten, Your Majesty."

"You have your Queen's gratitude. My dogs are precious friends." She smiled. "Your finger is bleeding. Take this." She wrapped the lace handkerchief round my finger. "There. A keepsake for a kind deed."

She rose to her feet and smoothed her skirts down as I leapt up and backed away, speechless, my eyes on the floor again. Walter's hand closed like a vice on my shoulder and steered me painfully out of the door.

And that was how I first met the Queen.

PAW-FECT PALS

Mary loved dogs, both hunting hounds and small lapdogs. It is said that when she was growing up in France, there were twenty-two pet lapdogs at the French palace!

One week later

Walter came and found me while I was sweeping out the hearth.

"Up you get," he growled. "You're finished here."

My heart sank down to the soles of my feet. I had been worried every day about being thrown out of the palace for daring to talk to the Queen. I'd starve on the streets.

"I'm sorry, sir. Please let me stay. *Please.* I never meant to talk to her."

"It's too late for that, boy. You *did* talk to her, so now you're out of the kitchen." As I fought back tears, I saw that he was smiling. "Though I dare say," he said, "we'll see you down here pinching all the best bits of meat for the beasts."

"What?"

"The Queen wants you to help look after her pets. You're to become royal dog keeper." He laughed at the look on my face. "You're a clever lad. See you make the most of this chance. Look after those dogs as if they were your own children – the Queen dotes on them."

An hour later I'd been scrubbed until my skin was nearly raw. My hair had been cut and my nails pared and I'd been fastened into a suit of dark green cloth that almost fitted me. Janet gaped as I went past the laundry door. I looked at my reflection in the still surface of a tub of water and hardly recognised myself. Alec the turnspit was gone. Alec the royal servant looked back at me.

TWO LASSES

When Mary was born and her father was told he had a daughter, not a son, he is supposed to have said:

"It cam wi' a lass and it will gang wi' a lass."

Which means: it began with a girl and it will end with a girl.

He was talking about the line of Stuart kings and queens, which began when Marjorie, daughter of King Robert the Bruce, married Walter Stuart (also spelled Stewart) in 1315. It did 'gang wi a lass', but not with Mary: the last Stuart ruler was Queen Anne, who died in 1714.

PALACE OF HOLYROODHOUSE

This is an English soldier's drawing of Edinburgh in 1544 showing the Palace of Holyroodhouse at one end of the town's main street, which is called the 'Royal Mile'. The words over the palace say: The Kyng of Skotes Palas (the king of Scots palace). The palace stands beside Edinburgh's dramatic hills, Arthur's Seat and Salisbury Crags, where Mary walked and rode.

2. THE QUEEN SETTLES IN

Palace of Holyroodhouse, Edinburgh
September 1561

I'd thought that the Queen had just the two dogs, Louis and Isabelle, but I soon discovered she loved animals and had quite a few. I'd little to do with the horses, or the hounds and hawks kept for hunting – they had their own servants. But as well as the little dogs, I took care of Philippe, a wee monkey who wore clothes; some song birds (linnets and such); and also

Hector the parrot, a big grey bundle of feathers with a great curved beak, who could speak French and Scots and Latin.

All this was nothing, the hawk master told me, compared with what they'd had in France. There had been a proper zoo in the French palace, with lions, a cheetah, camels, elephants and a giraffe. He showed me pictures in a book, but the animals looked to me as if someone had made them up, with their humpy backs and bendy noses and necks like ladders.

The Queen usually had the dogs with her in the evenings, and sometimes also Hector or Philippe, and I'd be called to take food to them or groom them or clean up after them. When I was in the Queen's chambers, I was tucked away in a corner and folk often forgot I was there, so I saw and heard a lot of things I probably shouldn't have.

The Queen usually passed the time with her ladies in waiting. They were often called 'the four Marys' because they were all named Mary! Then there was an Italian called

David Rizzio: he was the man I'd seen with the lute. He often played for the Queen and her guests as they talked or had a game of dice or cards. They also liked billiards, chess and backgammon. Sometimes there was dancing.

The Four Marys

When Mary left Scotland for France aged five, four girls the same age went with her to keep her company. All four were called Mary! (It was the most popular name for girls at that time.)

- ⚓ Mary Beaton
- ⚓ Mary Seton
- ⚓ Mary Livingston
- ⚓ Mary Fleming

They stayed her friends throughout her life and were known as 'the four Marys'.

They all returned to Scotland with Mary when they were eighteen. They ate with her, went hunting and hawking with her, danced and sang.

The ladies often sewed with the Queen – fine embroidery for hangings and bed covers, made with silk threads in the colours of a flower garden. Sometimes they sat quietly and read. I'd never dreamed the world *had* so many books. Queen Mary had a whole room full of them, in French and Latin, Scots and English, Italian, Spanish and Greek – or so I was told. They all looked the same to me, since I couldn't read. When the Queen found that out, she got one of her ladies to teach me.

When she was outdoors, the Queen loved to be active and everyone admired her horse riding and hunting. She liked archery, golf and croquet too.

Things to Do

- Attend a dance and be the best-dressed person in the room
- Long horse ride in Holyrood Park
- Play fetch with Isabelle and Louis
- Meet with a royal foreign visitor
- Attend church
- Play a game of backgammon with the four Marys
- Read a book about the new science of the stars
- Royal feasting!
- Finish my embroidery

MARYS IN DISGUISE

Some stories say that Queen Mary and the four Marys would wear disguises – sometimes even dressed as men – to go shopping in Edinburgh or St Andrews and pass unnoticed through the crowds.

The Queen had important visitors – nobles and suchlike. One of those was her half-brother, Lord James Stuart, who she made Earl of Moray. She often looked to him for advice. Some folk whispered *he* should rule Scotland, being a man and a Protestant. But even though James Stuart's father was King James V, the king hadn't been married to his mother, so James Stuart couldn't inherit the crown.

The Queen wanted to travel and see something of her country – and check that the lords of Scotland weren't up to anything behind her back. Janet came rushing up to me as we all hurried about packing chests and boxes.

"You'll never guess," she said, excitedly. "Mistress Semple says I'm to go with the Queen's servants to help look after Her Majesty's clothes. Isn't it grand?"

"Then we'll be company for each other," I said. "I'm going too, to look after Louis and Isabelle."

THE QUEEN ON TOUR

In the 1500s, kings and queens sometimes went 'on progress', which means on tour, around their kingdoms. Television and photography hadn't been invented yet, so tours let the people see their rulers.

The royal habits and clothes would become the new fashion for the well-off people who saw them. Being 'on progress' also allowed rulers to check that nobles were not plotting against them.

Mary Queen of Scots did a *lot* of travelling after her return to Scotland. Her whole court of servants and lords and ladies would go with her, staying in castles or large houses.

EXPENSIVE GUESTS!

When the Queen and her court were on tour, castle owners had to feed them all and provide entertainment!

The Queen's Lodgings, St Andrews, Fife, Scotland
October 1561

Janet and I were eating our breakfast.

"I never thought I'd see anything outside Edinburgh," I said. "Look at us – Linlithgow, Stirling, Perth, Dundee and now St Andrews!"

Janet grinned at me. "And I thought I'd have my hands in a washtub in Holyrood my whole life. But I'm allowed to mend some of the Queen's petticoats too – Mistress Semple says my stitches are neater than most of the proper seamstresses'. Oh, you should feel the velvets and silks, Alec. That must be what angels wear."

"Hurry up, you two!" came a shout, so we bolted the rest of our porridge in silence.

QUEEN MARY'S CLOTHES AND JEWELS

Mary loved fine clothing. In 1561, a list of her clothes included:

- 60 dresses
- 14 cloaks
- 34 petticoats

Mary often wore or carried a jewelled cross to show her commitment to her religion.

Mary lived long before sewing machines. Every stitch of lace or embroidery was hand sewn.

Mary often wore white, to look striking with her dark red hair. She also liked red and black: the most expensive dye colours.

Mary was nearly six feet tall – unusually tall for the 1560s.

Jewels help a queen seem impressive. Mary's favourites were pearls and rubies. She even used jewels as buttons!

Pieces of jewellery called pomanders held sweet-smelling herbs like lavender. In Mary's time, people didn't wash as much and there were no flushing toilets, so there were lots of bad smells!

WHAT TO WEAR IN THE 1500s

Rich women wore:

Headdresses, caps or veils. Women at the time often copied the head coverings in Mary's portraits.

Sleeves were detachable so they could be worn with different bodices and skirts.

Outer parts were slashed to show different fabric underneath.

Expensive clothes were brightly coloured, embroidered and trimmed with beads, lace or gems.

Women's clothes came in several separate parts:

ruff

bodice

sleeves

petticoat

skirt

A farthingale was a frame worn under skirts to create the right shape. Some were so big, wearers couldn't get through doors!

Rich men's clothes were every bit as fancy as women's. Rich men wore:

Even simple clothing was expensive for poorer people. They often had just one set to wear every day.

Poor people's clothing was undyed or in cheap dye colours such as green and brown.

hat

shirt (underneath)

ruff

sleeves

doublet

cloak

breeches

hose

shoes or boots

Expensive clothes were made from velvet, silk, linen or wool.

Poor people's clothes were only made from linen or wool.

Palace of Holyroodhouse, Edinburgh
March 1562

"I wish that she or I were a man. Then the two of us could marry and that would be an end to all these problems."

Queen Mary paced in front of the fire. Who could she be talking about? I stopped brushing Philippe the monkey so I could listen more closely.

She laughed. "Still, I doubt that God will grant me such a miracle, so I must content myself with a meeting, Maitland."

Maitland of Lethington was one of her advisors.

ELIZABETH I

"Queen Elizabeth wishes to meet you, and you wish to meet her. Now we have only to agree a time and place," replied Maitland.

Ah! She must mean Elizabeth of England, her cousin. What sorts of problems did Queen Mary want to solve with a marriage? What sorts of problems could she have? She was the Queen – everyone rushed to do her bidding. And she always seemed so carefree and full of play.

Philippe batted at the brush wanting more grooming, but I stayed completely still so I could hear the Queen talk on.

"A meeting is in both our interests," she said. "We live on the same island, speak the same language… We are each other's closest kinswoman. And we are both Queens."

"Mmmm." Maitland's response was uncertain.

"She sent me this ring," the Queen held out her hand, where a huge diamond glittered, "as a token of friendship. I have strong hopes that this meeting will bind us together in even greater friendship. She will see that I am no threat to her, and then she will name me her heir."

"Well madam, that is what we must hope for."

The Queen sounded bright and confident, but Maitland's voice was more doubtful.

And then that rascal Philippe bit me and I let out a yelp and got sent away, and I heard no more.

I wanted Queen Elizabeth to meet and love her cousin, and for all my Queen's problems, whatever they were, to be over.

The Scottish Reformation: What are Protestants and Catholics?

Until about 1500, Scotland, like the rest of Europe, was a Catholic country. But in Holland and Germany, people started saying the church was too wealthy and powerful. In 1525, a German priest called Martin Luther set up a new church. People who joined this church were called Protestants.

Both Protestants and Catholics are Christians and worship Jesus, but for Catholics the Pope is the head of the church and is appointed by God to interpret the Bible. Protestants believe that each Christian has their own relationship to God and can read the Bible for themselves.

Martin Luther's Protestant ideas spread to Scotland. So did those of another Protestant thinker, John Calvin, who thought monarchs shouldn't have anything to do with running the church. The Scottish Catholic church began to execute reformers, but the new religion grew anyway. By the time Mary returned from France, Scotland was officially Protestant, although there were still many Catholics, especially in the Highlands.

Mary was Catholic, and some Scottish Catholics hoped she would side with them, but she tried to find a balance, appointing both Protestants and Catholics to important positions.

Mary and Elizabeth

Mary was convinced that if she and Queen Elizabeth could only talk face to face, rather than relying on messages, they would become friends.

Here is Mary's affectionate signature on one of her many letters to Elizabeth:

She has written: Your richt gud sister and cusignes Marie R.

This uses spelling from an earlier form of English. It means: Your right good sister and cousin, Mary R. (The R. is short for Regina or Rex, Latin for queen or king.)

Mary was Elizabeth's cousin. She is using the word 'sister' to say that they are both in the same situation, they are 'sister queens'; she is emphasising what they have in common.

But Mary had a strong inherited connection to the English throne as well as the Scottish one. Her grandmother, Margaret Tudor, was the sister of Elizabeth's father, Henry VIII of England. And many Catholics living in England would have preferred to have Catholic Mary as their queen, rather than Protestant Elizabeth.

Elizabeth wrote warmly to her Scottish cousin, but she didn't want to invite her too close.

The Huntly Rebellion, 1562

The Queen had trouble with rebellious Scottish lords during her whole reign. One of the first was the Earl of Huntly from north-east Scotland. He was angry because Queen Mary gave some land he thought was his to her half-brother James Stuart, the Earl of Moray.

Mary summoned the Earl of Huntly to come to her, but he refused and gathered his own army.

JAMES STEWART

The Queen, her half-brother and their forces quickly defeated Huntly's army near Aberdeen. The Earl of Huntly collapsed after the battle and died.

His dead body was taken to Edinburgh and put on trial!

GUILTY

Strangely, months after his death, Huntly's body was found guilty of treason.

3. A ROYAL WEDDING

Palace of Holyroodhouse, Edinburgh
Summer 1563

Janet grabbed my arm and hauled me into a doorway.

"Oh, Alec, there's been an awful row. I was in the Queen's room sewing a cap for Mary Fleming, and John Knox came in and began ranting at the Queen. Everyone must have forgotten I was in the corner and once it all started up, I was afraid to move." She took a breath.

"Believe me, the Queen was furious. 'Tell me, Master Knox: what have *you* to do with any marriage of mine?' she said.

"'You canna marry a Catholic. Scotland willna stand for it,'" Janet growled, imitating Knox, and then said to me, "I couldna believe he dared speak to the Queen like that."

Then she went on, "And Erskine of Dun tried to calm things: 'Any prince in Europe would be glad to marry a lady as fair as yourself. You need not—'

"But the Queen yelled at him to be quiet and I saw she was crying. And then she ordered Knox out!

"Well, Mary Fleming held the door for him, looking daggers, and, as Knox went past, he said, 'All your jewels and fine clothes willna save you when death calls for you.'

"I thought she would slap him, but she just slammed the door behind him. Then the Queen ordered *everyone* out except the Marys, but I was still stuck in the corner.

"'How I detest that man,' the Queen said. 'I will *not* have him tell me who I may and may not marry.'

"Mary Beaton said she shouldn't worry, that there was plenty of time to find a good husband who would be a good king, but the Queen said, 'No. I must find a husband soon. Scotland needs an heir to the throne.'"

'THE MOST DANGEROUS MAN': JOHN KNOX (1513–1572)

John Knox was a minister who started the Scottish Protestant church, which is called the Presbyterian church.

Knox had returned to Scotland from Europe in 1559 full of Calvin's ideas. He preached against Catholicism – and against female rulers.

JOHN KNOX

He had written a book aimed at the English Queen Mary Tudor, called *First Blast of the Trumpet against the Monstrous Regiment of Women*. Mary, Queen of Scots – a woman *and* a Catholic – was doubly dreadful in his view.

Mary described him as 'the most dangerous man in the whole of my realm'.

Janet and I looked at each other.

"She's right," I said. "I hear folk talking. They want a baby – a boy – so they know the crown'll be safe."

"And why should it not be safe with a woman?" replied

Janet angrily. "But no, the lords say she must marry and then of course her husband will be king and nobody will care about Queen Mary any more, except to produce babes. The men always get their way."

She sounded so fierce I was feared to say anything.

"And even if she wants to marry," Janet went on, "how is she ever to find a man who'll please everyone?"

Neither of us had an answer to that.

December 1564

"Alec, come and take Hector away. He talks too much and makes my head ache."

"Yes, madam." I persuaded Hector to step from his perch onto my arm, where he dug his claws in and glared at me. I took him to his perch in the outer chamber and left him settling in for a long sulk.

When I went back into the Queen's chamber, she was throwing a ball for Isabelle to chase and laughing with Davy

Rizzio and the other musicians, her headache forgotten, while Maitland of Lethington talked to Mary Fleming by the window. (We all knew Maitland wanted to marry Mary Fleming, although he seemed to think it was a secret.)

After a few minutes Queen Mary sent the musicians away, apart from Rizzio.

"Davy," she said.

"Yes, madam?"

"I have a new job for you."

"A new job? Does my music displease you, madam?"

"Not at all, Davy. But I have another task for you, when you are not playing for me. I wish you to be my secretary."

Rizzio looked delighted. "Madam, I would be honoured."

I saw the look on Maitland's face. He was furious.

"The lords won't like this one bit," I said to Janet later. "They already think Davy Rizzio's got too big for his boots."

WHO WAS DAVID RIZZIO?

David Rizzio was Italian and an excellent musician. Mary trusted his loyalty.

The Scottish lords thought Rizzio was an arrogant Catholic foreigner. He had an influential job as Mary's secretary, which they wanted for themselves.

February 1565

There was someone new among the friends and courtiers who kept the Queen company in the evenings: a tall young man. It wasn't often that Queen Mary found herself having to look up at a dance partner, and she seemed to enjoy it. He was handsome too, golden haired, a good dancer and a lute player. Davy Rizzio was annoyed about that.

The ladies found him charming. Only the dogs didn't like him, so neither did I, though Janet said I was just jealous. But he showed his teeth too much when he smiled, as if he might take a nibble of you to see if he liked the taste,

then come back for a bigger bite if he did. He was the Queen's cousin Henry, Lord Darnley, and it wasn't long before people started to whisper about him as a possible husband for the Queen. They certainly made a fine-looking couple, and Janet and I agreed that the Queen had fallen completely in love with him.

TALL AND HANDSOME

Soon after meeting him, Mary was said to describe Darnley as

'the lustiest and best-proportioned lang man I have seen.'

('Lang' is Scots for 'tall'.)

POSH WASH

It's said that Mary used to rinse her face in white wine because she thought it would keep her pale skin clear!

July 1565

Lots of folk told my mistress that she shouldn't marry Darnley. People said he was moody and proud and only out for himself. Queen Elizabeth, who had still not arranged a meeting with Queen Mary, was against the match and tried to summon Darnley back to England.

Despite all this advice, I'd never seen Queen Mary as determined about anything: she was so in love with Darnley that she ignored everyone and went ahead with the wedding. There were banquets and dancing and music all day in the palace, and coins thrown to the crowds outside. I got three pennies and felt rich – I'd never had *any* money of my own before.

CHOOSING A HUSBAND

Mary had an impossible task, trying to find a husband who was noble enough to marry a queen, and who would keep everyone happy. Catholics were worried she'd choose a Protestant, and Protestants were worried she'd choose a Catholic. Queen Elizabeth I said she might name Mary as heir to the English throne if Mary married the right man. But no man *was* right.

Possible Husbands

DON CARLOS

NATIONALITY: Spanish

WHO?: Heir to the Spanish throne

RELIGION: Catholic

GOOD POINTS:

- Spain was wealthy, so he could supply troops and money to protect Scotland (which was poor)
- Popular with Mary's Catholic relatives

BAD POINTS:

- Unpopular in Protestant Scotland
- Would upset the religious balance Mary had worked hard to achieve

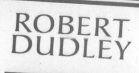

ROBERT DUDLEY

NATIONALITY: English

WHO?: English nobleman, Queen Elizabeth I's favourite

RELIGION: Protestant

GOOD POINTS:

- Might keep Elizabeth happy
- Might encourage Elizabeth to name Mary as her heir

BAD POINTS:

- Might not keep Elizabeth happy – she kept changing her mind
- Suspected of murdering his first wife!

HENRY DARNLEY

NATIONALITY: English/Scottish

WHO?: Mary's cousin

RELIGION: Changeable (Protestant in England, Catholic in Scotland)

GOOD POINTS:

- Would strengthen Mary's claim as Elizabeth's heir
- Good-looking

BAD POINTS:

- Would anger Scottish Protestants
- Would anger Elizabeth
- Unpopular choice with everyone – except Mary

Here I was with a job I loved, looking after dogs who loved me back, and I was practically part of a royal wedding. I could never have dreamed such a thing.

The Queen looked so happy, dancing with her new husband – King Henry, he was to be called now. I hoped they would be as happy as I was.

Queen Elizabeth's Worries

We already know that Mary had a strong claim on the English throne. Darnley was Mary's cousin, and he also had a fairly strong claim to be the next English king. Combined, their claim would be even stronger, as would be the claim of any children they might have.

Queen Elizabeth wanted to hold on to the English throne herself, so this marriage worried her.

Linlithgow Palace, Linlithgow, Scotland
December 1565

Janet and I were walking the dogs around Linlithgow loch. The Queen had been ill and was here to recover – or at least that's what we'd been told. Janet had made me swear not to tell anyone the truth.

"I heard her talking to Mary Beaton while I was in the room. I was letting out bodices for the Queen and now I know why – she's going to have a babe, Alec. Isn't it grand? A wee prince or princess."

"Ah, she'll be so happy with a babe, and the wee one will be Scotland's next king or queen. An heir to the throne at last," I agreed.

Folk might expect Darnley (I never got used to calling him King Henry) to be with the Queen at such a time, but he was away hunting. Again. He was in an almighty sulk because Parliament wouldn't give him the Crown Matrimonial.

"But he's got a crown," I'd said to Walter, puzzled.

"Aye, but this one would make him the Queen's equal in power, and he'd be sole ruler if she died. You'd go a long way before you found anyone who thinks *that's* a good idea," he replied.

The Queen and Darnley had hardly spent any time together in the past couple of months. The courtiers whispered behind his back about how vain and useless he was, and if the Queen overheard them, instead of getting angry with them, she just looked sad. I think she secretly agreed. I'd heard him pressing her again and again about this crown thing before I knew what it meant. However many times she

told him it wasn't up to her, a few days later he'd be at her again. The dogs and I had been right to distrust him. I hoped things would be better once the babe came, but I doubted it.

Problems seemed to be piling up like winter clouds round my mistress. She wanted for nothing and yet she had nothing that was truly her own: Darnley avoided her, the lords plotted behind her back, everyone wanted favours – land or power or a title. We servants hoped Elizabeth of England would do something to support her...

I feared for my Queen.

UNEXPECTED WATER FEATURE

Beautiful Linlithgow Palace was built by Mary's Scottish ancestors, the Stuarts. The oldest surviving fountain in Britain, commissioned by Mary's father, still stands in its courtyard. It is said that on Mary's parents' wedding day, the fountain flowed with wine!

4. MURDER!

Palace of Holyroodhouse, Edinburgh
10 March 1566

I was in Queen Mary's chambers because she and her supper-party guests were playing with the wee dogs. Isabelle had a litter of puppies, and the lords and ladies were picking them up, laughing at their floppy ears and silly ways.

Queen Mary sat in a big cushioned chair. Her baby was due in the summer, and she looked a bit weary. David Rizzio was playing the lute – something he hadn't often done since he was made secretary and got awful grand.

While Rizzio was playing, Darnley suddenly appeared up the stairs from his own apartments.

"Husband, come and join us," the Queen said, though she looked as surprised as everyone else. Darnley hadn't attended her parties for months.

He mumbled something no one could hear and, instead of sitting down, flitted around the chamber like a mayfly, picking things up, putting them down, glancing at the door, never settling.

"Is something wrong?" the Queen asked.

He shook his head, but that very second, someone else came up the same stairs: Patrick Ruthven, one of the Scottish lords who had always been close to Darnley. He was wearing armour and everyone gaped at him, for you didn't come into the Queen's apartments dressed for a fight.

"Your Majesty," he said. "Davy Rizzio must come with me. He has been here too long."

"What do you mean? How dare you speak to me like this." The Queen stood up, furious. "Darnley, what do you know about this?"

Darnley just shrugged.

Ruthven gestured at Rizzio and addressed the Queen: "That man has too much influence on you."

Now the Queen's servants woke up from the daze they had been in and moved towards Ruthven.

"Get your hands off me," Ruthven roared, though no one had touched him, and at that another five men burst into the room, waving pistols and daggers. The ladies screamed, and Rizzio ran behind the Queen to hide, holding on to her skirts. Isabelle was barking like a mad thing, and I ran to grab

her as one of the intruders aimed a kick at her.

They dragged Rizzio away from the Queen and into the other room. Isabelle broke free and ran after them, yapping. The servants shouted, but were afraid to follow. It was mayhem.

I could hear Rizzio screaming for help. "Save me! Save me madam, save my life!" and then there were terrible noises.

After a couple of minutes, the noise stopped and we heard the intruders clattering down the far stairs. The Queen sent one of her lords through to the other room to see that they had really left.

He came back looking grim. "They've gone, madam."

"And Davy Rizzio?"

He hesitated. "There's a trail of blood as though a body has been dragged away."

I heard an animal whimpering. Isabelle! Was she hurt? Without thinking, I rushed into the other room, and stopped dead. There was blood all over the floor, and in the middle of it stood Isabelle, her coat patched red. I picked her up, worried that she was hurt, but I soon realised that none of the blood was hers, and crept back to rub her down and put her with her puppies.

I saw that Darnley was still standing by the window. He looked as if he might be sick. The Queen turned from her visitors and rounded on him, furiously.

"What have you done, husband? Did you mean me to die – with our unborn child as well? You wicked man. What harm has Davy Rizzio ever done you? Get out of my rooms!"

He slunk off like a whipped dog as one of the servants came to tell the Queen that Rizzio was dead. She wept then, and was comforted by her ladies. A few minutes later she dried her face and said calmly, "No more tears now; I will think upon revenge."

I SPY (NOT)

Some of the Scottish lords who disliked David Rizzio said that he was a spy for the Pope (the head of the Catholic church)! There was no evidence for this at all.

Who Can Mary Trust?

Rizzio had been stabbed 57 times and Mary believed that the conspirators had planned to also kill her and her unborn child, so that her husband Darnley could take the crown. She realised she was in danger and escaped to Dunbar Castle.

Her supporters flocked to her. She returned to Edinburgh a week later with an army of 8,000. Frightened by this strength, the conspirators fled, and Darnley swore loyalty to Mary once more.

But who could the Queen trust?

Darnley	Wanted the crown for himself
David Rizzio	Dead
James Stuart, Earl of Moray, her half-brother	Rebelled after Mary married Darnley
Many Scottish lords	Conspired against Rizzio
Queen Elizabeth	Still avoided meeting; still angry at Mary's marriage

One of the few lords who seemed reliable was James Hepburn, Earl of Bothwell. He was the Lord High Admiral of Scotland. Mary had first met him in France, and he was one of her least troublesome lords.

Earl of Bothwell	Can he be trusted?

A Future King

Mary gave birth to a son, James Charles, on 19 June 1566 at Edinburgh Castle (which she felt was more secure than Holyrood Palace). There was great rejoicing at the safe arrival of this new Scottish prince, a direct heir to the throne.

Later that year, baby James was taken to Stirling Castle, where royal babies were usually brought up. He was cared for by the Erskine family while Mary was in Edinburgh.

Mary thought about him all the time and made plans for his safety.

JAMES & MARY

MAGIC MEDICINE

When Mary was giving birth to her son, one of her attendants tried to cast a spell to transfer her labour pains to another woman!

It didn't work.

Stirling Castle, Stirling, Scotland
December 1566

Janet and I managed to squeeze in right at the back of the chapel to watch little Prince James' baptism. He was six months old now, looking round at everything. And there was plenty to see: candles and torches, the Queen and her nobles in cloth of gold and cloth of silver. Only the Catholic lords were in the chapel – the Protestant nobles waited outside.

One of the godmothers was Queen Elizabeth of England. She wasn't there, but Queen Mary was delighted she had accepted the invitation to be a godparent. "You see?" I'd heard her say to her ministers. "This shows friendship to Scotland. And having Queen Elizabeth as a godmother will strengthen my son's claim to the English throne when Elizabeth dies." Elizabeth had sent a solid gold font as a baptism present and it glittered and gleamed

BAPTISM IN THE 1500s

At this time in Scotland, it was common for the priest to spit in the baby's mouth at a baptism! Mary refused this for little James, calling the archbishop a "pocky priest". She probably meant his skin had scars from smallpox.

in the light of the flames.

"I never thought I'd see something like this," I whispered to Janet.

"Nor me. It feels as if I'm living someone else's life." Janet's eyes were wide.

She was right. Here we both were, part of the Queen's household, with warm clothes and beds of our own and even a wee bit of money. I knew how to look after all sorts of animals now, and Janet did fine embroidery as well as sewing. We were servants but we knew as much about what was going on as many of the nobles, and we were able to see ceremonies like this one: the naming and blessing of a future king! We'd never be skivvies again.

After the baptism there was a great celebration with fireworks and masques and dancing. The Queen talked and laughed with one of her loyal lords, the Earl of Bothwell, and her half-brother James Stuart. She'd forgiven her half-brother for rebelling after her marriage.

It was a happy day for my mistress, but we all noticed that Darnley wasn't with her, even though he was staying in the castle somewhere. He and the Queen hardly spoke now.

Palace of Holyroodhouse, Edinburgh
10 February 1567

I wasn't long in bed when a great booming noise woke me from my sleep.

Earlier in the day, the Queen had paid a visit to church buildings in Edinburgh called Kirk O'Field. Darnley the King was staying there, recovering from an infection.

Then the Queen had come back to the palace to attend the wedding of two servants.

We'd all gone late to our beds, only to be woken by the incredible noise.

People rushed around in the dark, trying to find out what had happened, and then someone yelled, "The King! The King has

been blown up!" and pandemonium broke loose. At first, all was confusion: was Darnley injured? Was he dead? No one knew for sure.

But a little while later we learned that he really *was* dead. Strangled, and the house where he was staying had been stuffed with gunpowder and blown up!

Mutterings about murder began, for what else could it be? Who could have done such a thing? And had they meant to kill the Queen as well?

Calls for Justice

A drawing was made soon after Darnley's death to explain to a man called William Cecil what had happened. Cecil was gathering information about Scotland's court for Queen Elizabeth I.

At the top baby James is shown praying: "Judge and defend my cause, O Lord." (The murder is said to be 'his cause' because Darnley was his father.) Below that, the drawing shows the rubble after the explosion at Kirk O'Field. At the bottom, townspeople watch Darnley's body being carried away.

40 days later

After Darnley's murder, the Court went into mourning, all of us dressed in black and very gloomy. The Queen left

Edinburgh for a few days to recover a little, but rumours started up, saying that she'd known of the plot to kill her husband, that it was her revenge for the killing of David Rizzio.

I didn't believe a word of it: the Queen had been trying to reconcile with Darnley, and that's why he was in Edinburgh. But it was true that some of the nobles close to the Queen must have been involved with the plot. At night I heard shouts in the streets accusing the Earl of Bothwell of the murder.

GOLF GOSSIP

Mary was said to have enjoyed golf and there were rumours she played on the oldest links in the world at St Andrews days after Darnley died. This seemed uncaring, and led people to ask if she was involved in the murder.

But the golfing rumour is probably not true, because it came from Mary's enemies.

A Letter from Queen Elizabeth

Queen Elizabeth of England was so shocked at the murder of a king that she wrote to Mary immediately, calling on her to ensure that Darnley's death was avenged. Her letter implied that if people didn't see justice being done, they would blame their Queen and think that she was involved or was covering up for the murderer.

Elizabeth wrote to Mary in French. Here is a translation of part of the letter:

> My ears have been so astounded and my heart so frightened to hear of the horrible and abominable murder of your husband and my own cousin that I have scarcely spirit to write: yet I cannot conceal that I grieve more for you than him. I should not do the office of a faithful cousin and friend, if I did not urge you to preserve your honour, rather than look through your fingers at revenge on those who have done you that pleasure as most people say. I counsel you so to take this matter to heart, that you may show the world what a noble princess and loyal woman you are.

The letter still exists in the British National Archives.

Palace of Holyroodhouse, Edinburgh
April 1567

We went to Stirling, so that the Queen could visit little Prince James. The Queen took the dogs and also Philippe the monkey to amuse the baby, so I went too.

Wee James is a well-grown lad; he was keen to be up on his feet. He laughed at Philippe, pointing at his clothes and watching his antics, and he crawled about with the dogs, who didn't know what to make of him at all.

Queen Mary was pale and quiet, except when she was with her son. She was still much distressed after Darnley's murder.

Since he was found not guilty of the murder, Lord Bothwell has buzzed round my mistress like a wasp round a jam pot. Rumour is that he wants to marry her. I can't imagine that will happen. He *has* been loyal to her – unlike many of the lords of Scotland – but folk are still suspicious of him.

On the way back to Edinburgh, we spent the night at Linlithgow. I always love staying there; it's a peaceful place, with the swans sailing on the loch below the palace windows.

Next morning, a strange thing happened as we rode towards Edinburgh. Bothwell suddenly appeared, saying there was some sort of danger in Edinburgh and insisting that the Queen go with him to Dunbar Castle for her safety. The rest of us travelled on.

But there was no sign of any danger in Edinburgh. Goodness only knows if there ever had been, and yet the Queen was now shut up in Dunbar with Bothwell.

Kidnapped?

There has always been disagreement about exactly what happened when Mary rode off to Dunbar with Bothwell.

Was she tricked and kidnapped? Or did she go willingly?

Had she and Bothwell planned the meeting? Or did he take her by surprise?

Once she had spent the night alone with him, she had little choice but to marry him. In those times, women who stayed with men when they weren't married were regarded as no longer worthy of respect.

There was a problem – Bothwell was already married. But he wasn't going to let that stand in the way of becoming king. He divorced his wife, and married Mary two weeks later...

DUNBAR CASTLE TOO STRONG

Dunbar Castle was one of the strongest fortresses in Scotland. After Mary's reign, the Scottish Parliament ordered that it be "cast down utterly to the ground and destroyed", because it gave too much strength to whoever owned it!

Mary the Mermaid: Losing Loyalty

Mary had been a popular ruler when she first arrived in Scotland from France. But in 1567 opinion began to turn against her. The murders of Rizzio and Darnley gave her enemies many opportunities to start rumours about her. Ordinary people didn't know what to believe.

A pamphlet was pinned up around Edinburgh in 1567 by someone trying to ruin Mary's reputation.

It was one of the first political pamphlets in Scotland, and uses pictures because most people couldn't read.

M.R. stood for Mary Regina, or Queen Mary.

The picture suggested that Mary was a mermaid, luring men to their deaths! The person who drew it thought Mary had been involved in murder and hadn't kept her marriage vows, so was not a person deserving respect.

The letters I and J were regarded as the same letter, so I.H. stands for James Hepburn (Lord Bothwell's name). He is shown as a nervous hare, fearing swords of justice: the illustrator is suggesting he is guilty of a crime.

Palace of Holyroodhouse, Edinburgh

May 1567

It was another royal wedding day, but this one was very different to the Darnley marriage. There was no joy, just worry. The Queen was marrying the Earl of Bothwell and she looked ill and sad, like a widow, not a bride. There was no music in the palace now.

Janet and I watched from the back of the Great Hall as the ceremony took place – a Protestant one, this time. There were no masques or dancing or throwing of coins afterwards.

"The Queen never even had a new gown to wear," said Janet. "It couldn't be more different from last time."

I was afraid for the Queen. Her advisors had deserted her, and many of her ladies were gone. She seemed so alone, even with a new husband at her side.

15 June 1567

Some of the nobles were now openly rebelling against the Queen. She and Bothwell left Edinburgh for their safety.

When we heard that they were gathering men to fight against the rebel lords, half a dozen of us from

Holyroodhouse decided to sneak out to Carberry Hill, a few miles east, and join their army. I was sixteen, old enough to be a soldier.

I had to admit that Bothwell was a brave man. As we stood facing the rebel lords, he offered to fight in single combat, but no one took up the challenge.

OLD BATTLE, NEW BATTLE

Mary's army took their position on Carberry Hill in an entrenchment that had been created by the English army during the Rough Wooing.

I thought there would be a battle then, and feared it would go badly because so many men had been leaving us.

Queen Mary was desperate to avoid any fighting, and she was persuaded by her opponents that they meant her no harm. So she did the bravest thing I've ever seen. She walked calmly into the camp of the rebel lords.

"Do not worry," she told us as she left. "My lords are loyal to the crown. We will go back to Edinburgh and Parliament will meet and decide how we should proceed." Even then it looked like madness to most of us, but what else could she do, outnumbered as she was? She did not want to send her forces to be slaughtered. All was lost, and not even a blow struck in anger.

The rebel soldiers shouted terrible things at the Queen.

There is no honour in Scotland, I thought as I heard them. She believed they would treat her like the Queen she was, but they made her their prisoner, took her back to Edinburgh and held her captive.

And then they took her to Lochleven Castle.

5. LOCHLEVEN: A CASTLE PRISON

Lochleven Castle, Fife, Scotland
October 1567

The oars dipped and splashed and the boat slowly drew towards the island. Isabelle stood with her paws on the edge of the boat, tongue lolling, watching the water slip past. The poor dog had been pining for her companion Louis, who had died the month before, and her puppies had all grown up and found homes. I hoped this change might cheer her up.

The island and its castle loomed forbiddingly ahead. It was the home of the Douglases, but it certainly looked like a prison. I wondered if I had done the right thing, volunteering to join my mistress here. Ah well, too late. I felt a long way from home, and I suppose I was.

It began to rain just as the boatman tied up at the jetty. We gathered our bags and I helped the Queen's loyal lady Mary Seton and Janet onto the slippery wood. Isabelle stayed close, uneasy in this new place.

Mary Seton shivered, then straightened and walked towards the castle entrance, head high. Janet and I tried to follow her example.

"Take us to the Queen at once," she said to the gatekeeper.

We were led past a guard at the bottom of a round tower, and up its stairs. The gatekeeper gestured towards a door and left us. Mary Seton knocked, then we went in.

The Queen sat writing at a little table placed to catch the

light from a narrow window in the enormously thick stone walls. When she saw Mary Seton she leapt from her chair and ran to embrace her. "Mary! I am so glad they have let you come to me. And Alec and Janet, and dear Isabelle. Oh, my faithful servants, see what I am reduced to." She looked pale and thin, but still every inch a queen, and her eyes shone.

I no longer regretted my decision to come. The castle was a dour place, and walking Isabelle would be dull on such a small island, but I could put up with it knowing that our presence made a difference to the Queen.

"Tell me, Mary," said the Queen. "Is there any news of... of rescue?"

"You must be patient, madam. You still have loyal supporters, but they are outnumbered and cannot make a move yet."

The Queen sighed, then nodded. "And we have friends here." She lowered her voice. "George Douglas is sympathetic to me, as is his young cousin, Will." She turned to me. "Alec, I trust you to win Will completely to our side."

"I'll do my best, madam," I assured her.

Mary Gives Up Being Ruler

Soon after she came to Lochleven Castle, Mary's enemies forced her to abdicate, which meant signing a document giving up the throne.

Her baby son James was crowned King of Scotland, and her half-brother James Stuart was appointed regent, which meant he would rule until the king was old enough.

A Castle on an Island

Lochleven Castle sat on a small island in the middle of a wide inland loch, and was home to the Douglas family. The only way to get on or off the island was by boat, so it was ideal for preventing escape.

Mary was imprisoned there in June 1567, after being captured by rebel Scottish lords at Carberry Hill. One of these lords, Sir William Douglas, owned Lochleven Castle, and he acted as her jailer. His family, including his brother George and his young cousin Will, also lived at the castle.

THE PERFECT VIEW

A hundred years after Mary was imprisoned in Lochleven Castle, it was bought from the Douglas family by a gentleman architect called Sir William Bruce. Sir William thought the castle was far too old to live in and he built a new house on the loch shore – he just wanted the castle as a decorative feature to view from his garden!

November 1567

The Queen had already charmed Will Douglas. All I did was draw him closer by asking him to help look after Isabelle. He loved dogs and there were few animals on the island other than the birds that flock to Loch Leven. The skies were full of geese and their mournful calls. Will and I threw sticks for Isabelle on the short walk around the island shore. The Queen wasn't free to do even that. How she hated being cooped up.

After what sounded like a terrible few weeks when she first arrived, Queen Mary had gained the loyalty and affection of many of the Douglases. The young people, including Will, were often in her chambers.

Now we had joined her, she spent most days talking and embroidering with Mary Seton, with Janet stitching quietly nearby.

Gradually, the restrictions on the Queen eased. She ate with the Douglas family and was sometimes allowed on walks.

Unlike us, Will went back and forth from the island to the far shore. As the Douglases relaxed, Mary gave him letters to smuggle out. And he wasn't the only one willing to risk his family's anger.

"George Douglas is definitely in love with her," Janet said to me one day. "He'd do anything for a smile. The Queen doesn't exactly encourage him, but she doesn't put him off either. She'll need his help if she's going to escape."

"Have you noticed she never mentions Bothwell?"

Janet spat on the ground. "That's for Bothwell."

WHAT HAPPENED TO BOTHWELL?

After fleeing Carberry Hill, Bothwell set sail for Norway. Unfortunately for him, he was a wanted man there too and was captured. He was imprisoned in terrible conditions for the rest of his life, and died in 1578.

His mummified body is still on display in a church in Denmark.

ESCAPE PLANS THAT WENT WRONG

Mary attempted to escape Lochleven Castle a number of times, but her plans failed.

Once, she dressed as a washerwoman, but the boatman she asked to take her across the loch spotted her white hands. The real washerwoman's hands were red and chapped from working.

Another plan involved climbing the castle walls, which were over 2 metres high, but when they practised, Mary's lady in waiting fell and injured herself, so the plan was discovered.

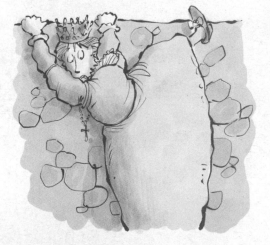

April 1568

Christmas came and went, spring arrived, and we were still on the island. The Queen struggled with all the frustrations of being restricted, and we tried to keep her spirits up.

Will took me out on the loch in a rowing boat and taught me to fish, and I told him tales of the early days of the Queen's reign, when everything had seemed made of light and music and hope. In the boat we could talk freely about plans for my mistress's escape. George Douglas was cooking something up with Mary Seton's brother, George Seton.

"We can't fix a date yet," said Will. "But we hope that the May Day revels will give us a chance to spirit the Queen away."

"How is she going to get out of a locked castle without being seen?"

He hesitated. "We haven't worked that out yet." He grinned. "Trust me – I won't let her down."

2 May 1568

May Day came and the castle was full of noise and confusion and celebrations. Will was doing all sorts of daft things, messing about with the boats and making the Queen follow him around like a servant while he pretended to be a king, in the manner of May Day parties.

Janet came to me, furious. "He's been drinking. He's going to ruin the plan, whatever it is."

The Queen went to lie down in her room, exhausted from tripping around at his heels, and I managed to corner Will on his own.

"What are you playing at, you fool?" I hissed as I pulled him into a corner.

His stupid expression dropped from his face like a mask. "I'm not drunk."

"You smell like a brewhouse."

"I spilled beer all over my clothes on purpose. Do you think I'd risk everything?" He looked angry now, and I saw that I'd made a mistake.

"I'm sorry," I said. "You were too convincing for me."

He grinned. "Good. If I can fool you, I should be fooling most folk. The boats are sorted – there's only one of them that won't sink before it reaches shore. I just need to get the keys off Sir William at suppertime and then..." He took a deep breath. "We'll be away, God willing."

"I wish I could come."

"So do I. But you and Janet and Mary Seton must be here to keep them from being suspicious for as long as possible."

"I know. We'll play our part."

At suppertime that evening, the castle was still full of bustle and disorder. The Queen, dressed in a servant's cape, paced the floor of her chamber, with Isabelle trotting at her heels. I swear the dog looked as anxious as her mistress. Now everything depended on whether Will could get the keys to the castle gate. Janet watched from the window.

"There!" she said suddenly. "The signal from Will. He's in the courtyard." She turned in a whirl of skirts. "It's time to go, madam."

The Queen embraced Mary Seton. "I will see you soon, my friend," she said, then turned to me and, to my shock, embraced me too. "My faithful Alec. Take care of my dogs until I can send for you. Farewell, dear Janet." She pulled her hood up and slipped out of the door.

We watched anxiously and saw her walk boldly between the revellers to where Will lounged against a wall near the gate, singing to himself. He must already have unlocked it, for the two of them disappeared through it in seconds.

Will's antics of the past day had worked: everyone in the courtyard had dismissed him as drunk and no one paid attention to him slipping away. A few minutes later, we saw a boat sliding through the dark water towards the shore, where

George Douglas and George Seton waited to take the Queen to freedom and safety.

Mary Seton, Janet and I had to go about our duties as if nothing had happened, until the next morning when word spread that the Queen was missing and we were all questioned over and over. There was great fury, and I feared for young Will once they found him.

Eventually they grew tired of keeping Mary, Janet and me, and decided to send us back to Holyroodhouse. It was a relief to leave the island; I was looking forward to reuniting Isabelle with some of her grown-up pups, to long walks, and to awaiting the return of the Queen to her proper place. She had been so brave! It made me smile to think how she'd escaped the Scottish lords, and I had high hopes of her regaining her throne.

THE ESCAPE FROM LOCHLEVEN CASTLE

Step 1: Young Will Douglas organises May Day celebrations and pretends to be drunk.

Step 2: He scuppers all of the boats (except one!)...

Step 3: ...and steals the castle keys as he pours the wine at supper.

Step 4: Mary disguises herself as a servant and waits in her rooms.

Step 5: When everything is ready, Will gives Mary the signal...

Step 6: Mary and Will walk out of the gates – unseen!

Step 7: Will rows Mary across the loch to George Douglas, waiting on shore with 200 horsemen. They escape!

A QUICK GUIDE TO MARY'S THREE HUSBANDS

1. FRANCIS II OF FRANCE

- Young French prince, then King of France
- Fragile health
- Engaged when Mary was 5 and Francis was 4, to bind Scotland and France
- Married at 14 (Mary was 15), died age 16
- Grew up alongside Mary

2. HENRY STUART, LORD DARNLEY

- Mary's cousin, had a claim to the English throne
- Born in Yorkshire
- Tall, handsome
- Married at 19 (Mary was 22), murdered age 21
- Vain, difficult, involved in murder of Rizzio

3. JAMES HEPBURN, EARL OF BOTHWELL

- Lord High Admiral of Scotland
- 12 years older than Mary, a close advisor
- Suspected of involvement in Darnley's murder
- Forced to flee Scotland
- Imprisoned in Denmark and died there

6. INTO ENGLAND

Palace of Holyroodhouse, Edinburgh
May 1568

News reached us in scraps: the Queen was gathering supporters and marching with them towards Dumbarton Castle; she had 6,000 soldiers against her half-brother's 4,000; there had been a battle; there had been no battle.

I begged leave to join her and fight for her, but they wouldn't let me go. Look after the dogs, they said.

And then we heard the news of Langside.

THE BATTLE OF LANGSIDE

Having escaped Lochleven Castle, Mary needed to assert her right to the throne over her half-brother, Regent Moray, and other Protestant lords. People flocked to join Mary's army, until it was much bigger than Regent Moray's, and they set off for the strong position of Dumbarton Castle on the Firth of Clyde.

But while Mary's army marched, her half-brother's men cleverly took cover among the cottages, hedges and gardens of a village called Langside that lay in their path. When Mary's army passed through, they were exposed. The earl in charge of Mary's army didn't have a battle plan, and the fight soon turned against the Queen.

When Mary tried to rally her commanders, they were so busy quarrelling among themselves that they ignored her, and in 45 minutes the battle was over. One hundred of Mary's soldiers were dead and over three hundred captured. Only one of her half-brother's soldiers had been killed.

The battle was a disaster for Mary and her followers.

FAINT STRATEGY

Mary's commander at the Battle of Langside, the Earl of Argyll, seemed to have no strategy, and perhaps relied simply on having the most soldiers. There is a report that he fainted during the fight, though this may be a rumour started by his enemies.

May 1568

I'd been looking everywhere for Janet to tell her the news. "The Queen has fled to England."

"What? Why would she do that? The English Queen is no friend to her."

I shrugged. "I know. It would have been better to stay in Scotland and try to rally support, or head for France – she's got relatives there who might help her."

Queen Mary hadn't listened to advice. She had cut off her beautiful red hair so she wouldn't be recognised, and sailed across the Solway Firth into England.

ELIZABETH'S PROBLEM

Mary's in my country now. Shall I...

A	...help a Catholic queen fight against Protestants in her country?	Not a good look for a Protestant queen.	✗
B	...just send her back to Scotland?	Without protection Mary will likely be killed, and that's not a good look either.	✗
C	...ask the French to come to Scotland and help her?	French troops might make their way into England.	✗
D	...leave her free to wander about my kingdom?	But the Pope believes Mary is rightful queen of England, so English Catholics will try to ditch me for her!	✗
E	...maybe just keep her quiet in a castle for a while...???	Hmmmm...	

Meanwhile Mary's enemies in Scotland and England conspired against her. She was accused again of involvement in Darnley's death. As regent, James Stuart, the Earl of Moray (Mary's half-brother) was enjoying the power he had long wanted. He joined the attempts to destroy Mary's reputation.

June 1568

Mary Seton, ever faithful, went to join Queen Mary in Carlisle Castle, and the little news I had came in letters from her or from Will Douglas, who had stayed with the queen. Many boxes of my mistress's clothes, tapestries and fine plates were sent to her. No one seemed to be sure whether the Queen was an honoured guest or a prisoner. Then she was moved further from Scotland – and it became clear that she was a captive.

My poor mistress! What sorrows lay ahead of her.

November 1568

Those of us left behind were trying our best to carry on as we thought the Queen would have wanted, but the country was in uproar, with constant clashes between supporters of the Queen and supporters of her half-brother, Regent Moray.

The Casket Letters

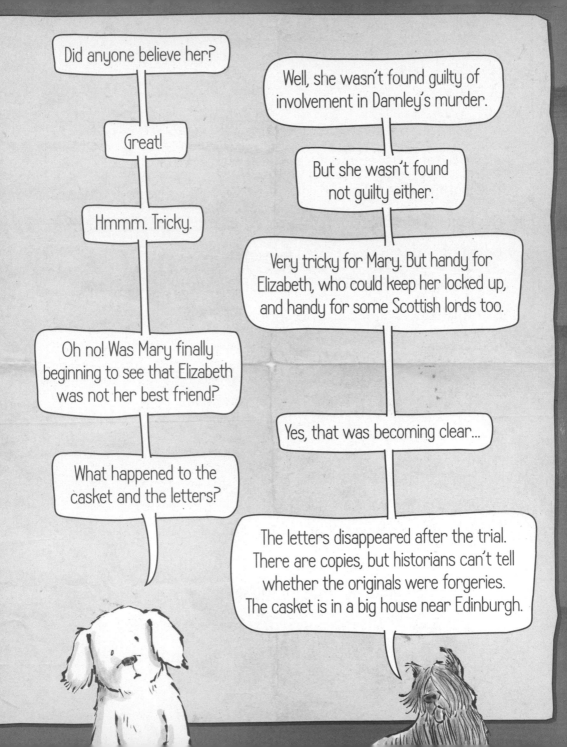

May 1569

Mary Seton warned me in one of her letters that it was becoming more difficult to get permission to write and, indeed, the letters from Will Douglas stopped altogether. The Queen, her staff and her boxes were moved from castle to castle, staying regularly with the Earl of Shrewsbury at Tutbury in Staffordshire. Mary Seton described Tutbury Castle as:

> ...a cold, damp castle, set on a hill and looking over a great marsh.

July 1569

We heard that Elizabeth of England had suggested to the Scottish lords that Queen Mary could live in England, or return to Scotland and rule jointly with her son, or even be restored to the throne herself, as long as the safety of Protestants and of Regent Moray were guaranteed.

Mary's Embroidery

Along with her letters, Mary's embroideries are important objects that tell us about her experience and thoughts.

During her long years of captivity, Mary passed the time with needlework. She would stitch with her companions and even with the ladies of the castles where she was captive, such as Bess of Hardwicke at Tutbury. She loved to put symbols and hidden messages into her needlework.

A famous piece shows a ginger cat tormenting a mouse. The cat, with its claws trapping the mouse tail, is thought to represent Elizabeth I, and the mouse to represent Mary herself.

I was full of hope – surely my mistress would soon return? But a few days later, Janet ran outside to where I was exercising the dogs, her face dark with anger.

"I've heard the talk upstairs – I came to tell you right away. The lords have voted against it. They won't have her back."

I couldn't believe it. "You can't mean they voted against *all* the ideas?"

Janet swiped away a tear. "All of them. You know what this means, don't you?"

I nodded. "Elizabeth won't let her go without the lords' agreement. Queen Mary might never return."

We walked on in gloomy silence for a bit.

"What about us?" Janet said suddenly. "We're the Queen's servants. There's no place for us here without her."

I'd been thinking that as well. It sounded disloyal, but we had to look to our own futures; there was nothing we could do to help the Queen.

IN STITCHES

Mary's embroidery often shows real and mythical animals, including a tiger, snails, a phoenix, a unicorn and what Scottish people then called a *shell-puddock*, which means a toad in a shell – a tortoise!

IMPRISONING A QUEEN

The Earl of Shrewsbury complained about the expense of keeping Mary and her servants, saying that their wine, spice and fuel were costing him £1,000 a year – a huge sum in those days.

"There are surely lots of fine ladies who need a skilled needlewoman like you in their household." I said. "What about Mary Fleming? She must have near as many dresses as the Queen."

"Maybe," said Janet, looking a bit cheerier. "And what about you?"

"I don't know. But I can read, I know how to look after all sorts of animals – I wouldn't be able to do *any* of those things if the Queen hadn't noticed me back when I was a young lad. I'd still be skivvying in the kitchen. I'll find something. And I'll make sure I can keep the dogs with me; no one else here cares anything about them."

The lords fought over the crown like wolves at a sheep carcass. None of them was fit to rule. Although she had made mistakes, the Queen had always wanted the best for her country and her people. Even in exile, even a prisoner, my mistress was more of a monarch than any of the lords of Scotland.

All I could do was pray for her.

January 1570

I heard today that Regent Moray, James Stuart, was shot dead in Linlithgow. I did not mourn him – he had repaid the kindness and trust of his half-sister the Queen by betraying her.

Mary's Long Captivity

Mary was held prisoner in English castles for nineteen years.

Queen Elizabeth never agreed to the meeting that Mary had sought for so long.

Once she entered England after racing away from the Battle of Langside, Mary was never able to return to Scotland.

THE MEETING THAT NEVER WAS

Sometimes films, plays and images show Mary and Elizabeth together, but these are fiction. Despite years of writing to each other, and Mary begging for a meeting, the two queens never actually saw one another face to face.

The same is true for Mary and her son James: there are paintings showing them together, but Mary was never able to see him again after she left Scotland when he was a baby.

MARY AND HER SON JAMES

7. PLOTS AND CODES

One of Mary's ciphers (codes) for writing secret letters

PLOTS AND FEAR OF PLOTS

Over the years of Mary's captivity, Queen Elizabeth of England grew increasingly fearful that the Scottish queen was plotting against her. She gave orders to those holding Mary to keep a closer watch on her: Mary's few freedoms became more and more limited. The number of Mary's servants was also reduced. She had been served by her own maids, grooms and cooks, but most of these were sent home. Mary Seton became unwell and retired to France in 1583.

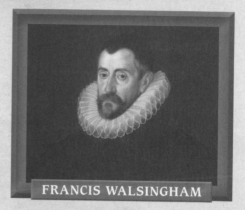

FRANCIS WALSINGHAM

As Queen Mary grew more isolated and more certain that Elizabeth would never release her, she placed her hope in various escape plots. She still had many supporters in the outside world who wanted to help her, both in Scotland and among English Catholics. But some of the escape plots involved people who were also calling for Elizabeth's murder, and that, of course, was a serious crime. Seeking to kill a king or queen is called 'treason'.

Queen Elizabeth had a trusted spymaster called Francis Walsingham. It was Walsingham's job to protect Elizabeth against any plots. He had a network of his own spies, informants and double agents. Though Mary didn't know, some of them worked as her servants and in the households where she was held captive.

SHHHH! SECRET SCHOOL

Queen Elizabeth's spymaster, Sir Francis Walsingham, started a spy school in London to train the spies who worked for him.

THE BABINGTON PLOT

1 By 1586, Mary was forbidden to write private letters to anyone. But a local brewer offered to smuggle out coded letters in a beer cask.

2 A Catholic Englishman called Sir Anthony Babington wrote to Mary this way, plotting to rescue her. Unfortunately, he was also plotting to kill Queen Elizabeth and so Mary became connected to the murder plot too.

3 Even more unfortunately, the beer cask was a trick by spymaster Walsingham! One of Mary's first letters explained the code, so he was able to read them all.

4 Walsingham had Sir Anthony Babington executed for treason, and Mary knew she would be next. But she wrote to a French cousin: *My heart does not fail me.*

CODED LETTER

Sir Anthony Babington and Mary wrote letters in code, using symbols and numbers to replace letters, common words and names.

Can you work out what this letter says using the code provided?

to	you	we	queen	Mary	Spain	Sir A. Babington
♣	ℵ	∂	∝	♥	◆	♠

A	B	C	D	E	F	G	H	I	J	K	L	M
ϒ	φ	}	ς	λ	ǀ	κ	ν	π	◊	≅	ρ	σ

N	O	P	Q	R	S	T	U	V	W	X	Y	Z
τ	ϖ	ω	ο	ξ	ψ	ζ	{	°	Θ	υ	~	μ

CODE LOAD

When the Babington Plot was uncovered, all Mary's papers were seized. They contained details of over 100 different codes she had used in her letters.

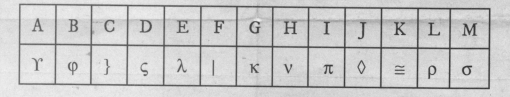

ς λ γ ξ ∝

_____ _____ _____ ♥ ,

ζ ν λ ξ λ   π ψ   ϒ   ω ρ ϖ ζ   ζ ϖ   ξ λ ψ } { λ   ℵ .

_____ __ _ _____ __ _____ _____ _____ .

Θ λ   Θ π ρ ρ   ψ λ λ ≡   ν λ ρ ω | ξ ϖ σ   ◆ .

__ _____ _____ _____ _____ _____ .

ℵ   Θ π ρ ρ   ψ ϖ ϖ τ   φ λ | ξ λ λ .

_____ _____ _____ _____ .

~ ϖ { ξ ψ | ϒ π ζ ν | { ρ ρ ~ ,

_____ _____ _____ ,

♠

_____ _ _____

Solution on p.127

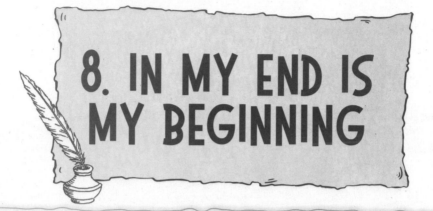

8. IN MY END IS MY BEGINNING

Marlin's Wynd, Edinburgh

February 1587

Dear Janet,

I can scarce believe it is five years since I last wrote to you. I can only hope you are still in Stirling and that this will reach you from Edinburgh, where I live and work still. You must know of the Queen's death, but there are many false rumours of what happened. I was there, and know the truth, and you should know it too.

I had a letter at the end of January, asking me to go to Fotheringhay Castle in Northamptonshire. It said the Queen was preparing for death and wanted me to come and collect her Skye terrier, Geddon.

When I got there, I met the Queen's remaining ladies. They warned me I would find her much changed, but it was still a shock. Nineteen years of illness and fear and imprisonment... I would scarce have recognised her but for her beautiful white hands. But she knew me.

"Alec? Is it you?" she said. "I had forgotten you would be a man grown."

I couldn't say anything — I was near to crying.

"No sadness for me, Alec. I am weary of this world. Do not grieve — rejoice for me that my suffering will soon end."

And then the wee dog came in and sniffed at my boots and we talked of cheerier things.

When the day of her execution came, the Queen's ladies and attendants and I were determined to be as brave as our mistress. She stood before us, calm, her prayer book in her fingers. That morning she looked every inch a queen, dressed in black satin, a white cap on her auburn hair, a long white veil, like a bride's, flowing to the floor behind her.

In the Great Hall, her ladies took off her cap and veil and dress. There was a gasp as the rest of us saw that, beneath the black dress, the Queen wore a crimson petticoat.

Our dear queen's eyes were then covered with a blindfold of white cloth, and she was left alone.

She showed no fear, knelt at once, felt with her hands for the block and laid her neck on it. "Into your hands, Lord, I commend my spirit," she cried.

And then the axe fell.

After the execution, I heard whining and Geddon came creeping out from the Queen's skirts, all covered in her blood, and trembling. The dog wouldn't stop howling. It knew something terrible had happened.

I took it home with me as the Queen had asked. The poor thing is quiet now, but pines for its mistress. I sit by the fire with it and still it shivers and howls.

I would howl myself, if I could. Instead I comfort the dog, and I look at the lace-edged handkerchief the Queen gave me the first time I met her, all those years ago. Until I go to my own grave she will be my gracious mistress, Mary, Queen of Scots.

I wish you strength to bear this grievous news, Janet. I know she was your gracious mistress too.

Your friend of old,

Alec

QUEEN'S BEST FRIEND

Mary had always loved dogs, and her Skye terrier Geddon was said to have hidden under her skirts as she went to her death, and sat by her body until it was carried away.

A FINAL SHOCK

When the executioner held up Mary's head by her famed red hair, it fell to the ground and people saw that the hair was a wig. Mary was 44 at the time of her death and her own hair was then short and grey.

MARY'S EXECUTION

Crimson was the colour of Catholic martyrdom. Mary's crimson petticoat symbolised her belief that she was being killed because she was a Catholic. Her pride in her faith gave her courage.

Elizabeth claimed that the execution had taken place without her consent, but since she had signed the death warrant, that wasn't very convincing.

There was unrest in Scotland as news of the execution spread, but rumours of war with England came to nothing.

A CHANT TO LEARN...

Children in Scotland have long chanted a short verse with a fun rhythm but a violent history:

Mary Queen of Scots got her head chopped off,

Head chopped off, head chopped off!

Mary Queen of Scots got her head chopped off,

Head. Chopped. OFF!

This rhyme is said when lopping the flowers or seed heads off dandelions, or as part of a playground game.

MARY'S SON: KING OF SCOTLAND AND ENGLAND

Mary's son James (King James VI of Scotland) had long been positioning himself as next in line to the throne of England after Queen Elizabeth's death. He had been raised a Protestant by the Scottish lords, and the English queen approved him as her heir.

So when Elizabeth I died in 1603, Mary's son was crowned King James I of England, and kept the throne of Scotland too. This brought Scotland and England together as jointly ruled countries, and it is called 'the Union of the Crowns'.

James had his mother's body moved from Peterborough Cathedral to Westminster Abbey, where it still lies in a white marble tomb very close to the tomb of Elizabeth I. The two cousin queens who never met are side by side in death.

Every British monarch since that time is descended directly from Mary. In this way, her motto – *In my end is my beginning* – came true.

JAMES VI AND I

In my end is my
beginning...

MARY, QUEEN OF SCOTS QUIZ

Once you've read the book, see what you can remember about Mary...

1. **Mary was born in...?**

   A. Edinburgh, Scotland

   B. London, England

   C. Linlithgow, Scotland

   D. Paris, France

2. **Mary's favourite pets were...?**

   A. Her horses

   B. Her small dogs

   C. Her French menagerie, including an elephant and a giraffe

   D. The cats in the palace kitchen

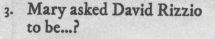

3. **Mary asked David Rizzio to be...?**

   A. Her secretary

   B. Her husband

   C. The court composer

   D. The royal dog keeper

4. **What is a pomander?**

   A. A breed of small dog

   B. A type of fruit

   C. A piece of jewellery

   D. A type of hair-styling cream

5. **What was Queen Elizabeth's christening gift to Mary's son, Prince James?**

   A. A solid gold christening font

   B. A solid gold high chair

   C. A set of solid gold spoons

   D. A solid gold rocking horse

6. **Mary's last husband was...?**

   A. Lord Darnley

   B. Francis Walsingham

   C. The Earl of Shrewsbury

   D. The Earl of Bothwell

7. **Who rowed Mary away from Lochleven Castle?**

   A. Will Douglas

   B. Alec Leslie

   C. George Seton

   D. George Douglas

8. **Which sport did Mary NOT take part in?**

   A. Golf

   B. Swimming

   C. Archery

   D. Horse riding

9. **Which animal did Mary use to represent Queen Elizabeth in her embroidery?**

   A. A mouse

   B. A rat

   C. A cat

   D. A dog

CODED LETTER SOLUTION (p.117)

Dear Queen Mary,

There is a plot to rescue you. We will seek help from Spain. You will soon be free.

Yours faithfully,
Sir A. Babington

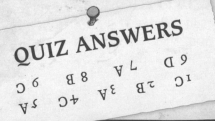

QUIZ ANSWERS

1C 2B 3A 4C 5A 6D 7A 8B 9C

Gill Arbuthnott used to be a biology teacher and now writes about microbes, the periodic table, space travel and fascinating facts from Scottish history. Her other book in the Factastic Facts series is *A Secret Diary of the First World War*. Gill lives in Edinburgh.

Mike Phillips has been drawing children's books full of pirate dogs, awful Egyptians and spy rats for more than twenty years. He's the illustrator of the *Museum Mystery Squad* and many books in the *Horrible Histories* and *Horrible Geographies* series. Mike lives in a small village in North Devon.

ACKNOWLEDGEMENTS

I am not a historian, so huge thanks to George Harris, who is, for his comments, clarifications and corrections. Any errors left are all my own work!

– G.A.